Vamos al circo, querido dragón

It's Circus Time, Dear Dragon

por/by Margaret Hillert

Ilustrado por/Illustrated by Jack Pullan

NORWOOD HOUSE PRESS

Querido padre o tutor: Es posible que los libros de esta serie para lectores principiantes les resulten familiares, ya que las versiones originales de los mismos podrían haber formado parte de sus primeras lecturas. Estos textos, cuidadosamente escritos, incluyen palabras de uso frecuente que le proveen al niño la oportunidad de familiarizarse con las más comúnmente usadas en el lenguaje escrito. Estas nuevas versiones han sido actualizadas y las encantadoras ilustraciones son sumamente atractivas para una nueva generación de pequeños lectores.

Primero, léale el cuento al niño, después permita que él lea las palabras con las que esté familiarizado, y pronto podrá leer solito todo el cuento. En cada paso, elogie el esfuerzo del niño para que desarrolle confianza como lector independiente. Hable sobre las ilustraciones y anime al niño a relacionar el cuento con su propia vida.

Al final del cuento, encontrará actividades relacionadas con la lectura que ayudarán a su niño a practicar y fortalecer sus habilidades como lector. Estas actividades, junto con las preguntas de comprensión, se adhieren a los estándares actuales, de manera que la lectura en casa apoyará directamente los objetivos de instrucción en el salón de clase.

Sobre todo, la parte más importante de toda la experiencia de la lectura es ¡divertirse y disfrutarla!

Dear Caregiver: The books in this Beginning-to-Read collection may look somewhat familiar in that the original versions could have been a part of your own early reading experiences. These carefully written texts feature common sight words to provide your child multiple exposures to the words appearing most frequently in written text. These new versions have been updated and the engaging illustrations are highly appealing to a contemporary audience of young readers.

Begin by reading the story to your child, followed by letting him or her read familiar words and soon your child will be able to read the story independently. At each step of the way, be sure to praise your reader's efforts to build his or her confidence as an independent reader. Discuss the pictures and encourage your child to make connections between the story and his or her own life.

At the end of the story, you will find reading activities that will help your child practice and strengthen beginning reading skills. These activities, along with the comprehension questions are aligned to current standards, so reading efforts at home will directly support the instructional goals in the classroom.

Above all, the most important part of the reading experience is to have fun and enjoy it!

Shannon Cannon

Shannon Cannon, Ph.D., Consultora de lectoescritura / Literacy Consultant

Norwood House Press • www.norwoodhousepress.com
Beginning-to-Read ™ is a registered trademark of Norwood House Press.
Illustration and cover design copyright ©2018 by Norwood House Press. All Rights Reserved.

Authorized Bilingual adaptation from the U.S. English language edition, entitled It's Circus Time, Dear Dragon by Margaret Hillert. Copyright © 2017 Margaret Hillert. Bilingual adaptation Copyright © 2018 Margaret Hillert. Translated and adapted with permission. All rights reserved. Pearson and Vamos al circo, querido dragón are trademarks, in the US and/or other countries, of Pearson Education, Inc. or its affiliates. This publication is protected by copyright, and prior permission to re-use in any way in any format is required by both Norwood House Press and Pearson Education.   This book is authorized in the United States for use in schools and public libraries.

LIBRARY OF CONGRESS CATALOGING-IN-PUBLICATION DATA
Names: Hillert, Margaret, author. | Pullan, Jack, illustrator. | Del Risco,
   Eida, translator.
Title: Vamos al circo, Querido Dragón = It's circus time, Dear Dragon / por
   Margaret Hillert ; ilustrado por Jack Pullan ; traducido por Eida Del
   Risco.
Other titles: It's circus time, Dear Dragon | It is circus time, Dear Dragon
Description: Chicago, IL : Norwood House Press, [2017] | Series: A
   beginning-to-read book | Summary: "A boy and his dragon go to the circus
   where Dear Dragon performs circus tricks and puts on a show of his own.
   Spanish/English edition includes reading activities"-- Provided by publisher.
Identifiers: LCCN 2016053227 (print) | LCCN 2017014211 (ebook) | ISBN
   9781684040346 (eBook) | ISBN 9781599538358 (library edition : alk. paper)
Subjects: | CYAC: Circus--Fiction. | Dragons--Fiction. | Spanish language
   materials--Bilingual.
Classification: LCC PZ73 (ebook) | LCC PZ73 .H55721172 2017 (print) | DDC
   [E]--dc23
LC record available at https://lccn.loc.gov/2016053227

Hardcover ISBN: 978-1-59953-835-8   Paperback ISBN: 978-1-68404-021-6

302N—072017
Manufactured in the United States of America in North Mankato, Minnesota.

Lo veo.

Lo veo.

¡Corre, corre, corre!

Esto es algo que nos va a gustar.

I see it.

I see it.

Run, run, run!

This is something we will like.

Mira eso.
Mira arriba, arriba.
Qué bonita.

Look at that.
Look up, up, up.
That is pretty.

Y aquí vienen los cómicos.
Mira aquí.
Mira, mira, mira.

And here come the funny ones.
Look here.
Look, look, look.

6

Ahora, mira aquí.
Oh, cielos.
Oh, cielos.
¿Qué es eso?

Now look here.
Oh, my.
Oh, my.
What is this?

Veo algo grande.
Grande, grande, grande.
Pero no veo a dragón.
¿Dónde está dragón?

I see something big.
Big, big, big.
But I do not see dragon.
Where is dragon?

9

Ay, no.
¿Qué veo ahora?
Ven aquí.
Ven aquí.
No puedes hacer eso.

Oh, no!
What do I see now?
Come here.
Come here.
You can not do that.

Ven conmigo.
¡Eres muy gracioso!
Pero no puedes hacer eso.

Come with me.
How funny you are!
But you can not do that.

Ahora tenemos que entrar aquí.
Aquí es donde está.
Ven y entra.

Now we have to go in here.
This is where it is.
Come on in here.

Este es un buen sitio para nosotros.
Mira lo que podemos ver.
Qué buen sitio.

This is a good spot for us.
Look what we can see.
What a good spot this is.

Ay, no.

¿Cómo llegaste hasta allá arriba?

Ese no es un buen sitio para ti.

Baja. Baja.

No vine aquí para verte hacer algo.

Te quiero aquí conmigo.

Oh, no!

How did you get way up there?

That is not a good spot for you.

Come down. Come down.

I did not come here to see you do something.

I want you here with me.

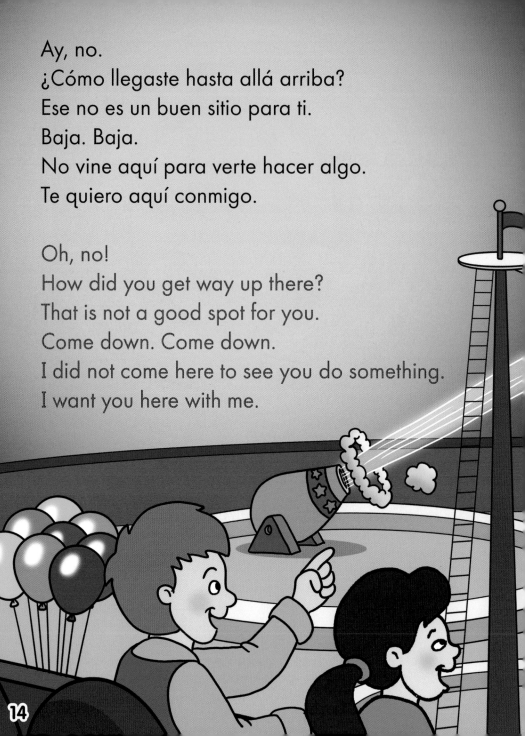

15

Y ahora, ¿qué es esto?
¿Qué es lo que veo?
¿En qué estás subido?

Now what is this?
What do I see?
What are you on?

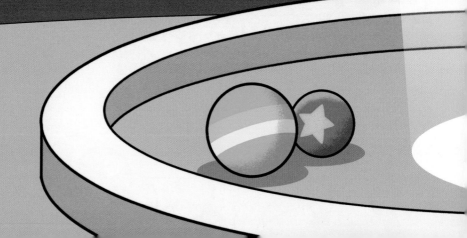

Eres bueno en eso.
Sí, eres muy bueno.
Pero te quiero aquí.
Ven aquí ahora.

You are good at that.
Yes, you are pretty good.
But I want you here.
Come here now.

Ahí no. Ahí no.
No hagas eso.
Quiero que vengas aquí conmigo.

Not there. Not there.
Do not do that.
I want you to come here to me.

Ay, ay.
Mírate.
Mira lo que tienes puesto.
Eres muy gracioso.

Oh, oh.
Look at you.
Look what you have on.
You are so funny.

Y ahora mírate.
Mira lo que puedes hacer.
Puedes ayudarla a saltar.
Caramba, ¡qué salto!

And now look at you.
See what you can do.
You can help this one jump.
My, what a jump!

Pero tenemos que irnos ahora.
Mamá y papá nos quieren de vuelta.
Vamos.
Tenemos que irnos.

But we have to go now.
Mother and Father want us.
Come on.
We have to go.

Aquí hay algo bonito.
Yo quiero el rojo.
Tú puedes tener uno también.

Here is something pretty.
I want a red one.
You can have one, too.

25

¡Mamá!
¡Papá!
Mírennos.
Miren lo que tenemos.

Mother!
Father!
Look at us.
See what we have.

Sí, sí.
Vemos lo que tienen.
Qué divertidos están.

Yes, yes.
We see what you have.
What fun for you.

27

Tú estás conmigo.
Y yo estoy contigo.

Here you are with me.
And here I am with you.

Ay, qué día tan feliz,
querido dragón.

Oh, what a happy day,
Dear Dragon.

The following activities support the findings of the National Reading Panel that determined the most effective components for reading instruction are: Phonemic Awareness, Phonics, Vocabulary, Fluency, and Text Comprehension.

Phonemic Awareness: The /t/ sound

Oddity Task: Say the /t/ sound for your child. Ask your child to say the word that doesn't have the /t/ sound in the following word groups:

tap, cap, pat	pod, pot, top	sip, pit, sit	pit, pat, pan
seam, seat, set	time, lime, tike	blue, to, stew	net, not, nod

Phonics: The letter Tt

1. Demonstrate how to form the letters **T** and **t** for your child.

2. Have your child practice writing **T** and **t** at least three times each.

3. Ask your child to point to the words in the book that have the letter **t** in them.

4. Write down the following words and ask your child to circle the letter **t** in each word:

not	too	not	little	to	that
get	want	this	what	tail	turtle

Vocabulary: Verbs

1. Explain to your child that words that describe actions are called verbs.

2. Write the following verbs from the story on separate pieces of paper:

run	look	see	come
go	get	do	help

3. Read each word to your child and ask your child to repeat it.

4. Mix the words up. Point to a word and ask your child to read it. Provide clues if your child needs them. Ask your child to describe him or herself using the verbs.

5. Read the following sentences to your child. Ask your child to provide an appropriate verb to complete the sentence.

- There is the circus tent, hurry let's (run) to get there fast.
- Can you (see) the big tent?
- (Look) over there! It's a circus parade.
- Would you like to (get) a balloon?
- There are so many things to (see/do) at the circus.
- It's time for us to (go) home.

Fluency: Choral Reading

1. Reread the story with your child at least two more times while your child tracks the print by running a finger under the words as they are read. Ask your child to read the words he or she knows with you.

2. Reread the story aloud together. Be careful to read at a rate that your child can keep up with.

3. Repeat choral reading and allow your child to be the lead reader and ask him or her to change from a whisper to a loud voice while you follow along and change your voice.

Text Comprehension: Discussion Time

1. Ask your child to retell the sequence of events in the story.

2. To check comprehension, ask your child the following questions:

- What were all the things Dear Dragon did that the boy did not want him to?
- What did Dear Dragon do to help in the circus?
- What was your favorite part of the story? Why?
- If you could be in a circus, what would you like to do? Why?

ACERCA DE LA AUTORA

Margaret Hillert ha ayudado a millones de niños de todo el mundo a aprender a leer independientemente. Fue maestra de primer grado por 34 años y durante esa época empezó a escribir libros con los que sus estudiantes pudieran ganar confianza en la lectura y pudieran, al mismo tiempo, disfrutarla. Ha escrito más de 100 libros para niños que comienzan a leer. De niña, disfrutaba escribiendo poesía y, de adulta, continuó su escritura poética tanto para niños como para adultos.

Photograph by Glenna Washburn

ABOUT THE AUTHOR

Margaret Hillert has helped millions of children all over the world learn to read independently. She was a first grade teacher for 34 years and during that time started writing books that her students could both gain confidence in reading and enjoy. She wrote well over 100 books for children just learning to read. As a child, she enjoyed writing poetry and continued her poetic writings as an adult for both children and adults.

ACERCA DEL ILUSTRADOR

Jack Pullan, ilustrador talentoso y creativo, es graduado de William Jewell College. También ha estudiado informalmente en la Universidad de Oxford y en el Instituto de Arte de Kansas City. Sus mentores han sido los renombrados acuarelistas Jim Hamil y Bill Amend. La obra de Jack ha adornado las páginas de numerosos y placenteros libros para niños, diversos materiales educativos y tiras cómicas, así como también muchas tarjetas de felicitación. Jack reside actualmente en Kansas.

ABOUT THE ILLUSTRATOR

A talented and creative illustrator, Jack Pullan, is a graduate of William Jewell College. He has also studied informally at Oxford University and the Kansas City Art Institute. He was mentored by the renowned watercolor artists, Jim Hamil and Bill Amend. Jack's work has graced the pages of many enjoyable children's books, various educational materials, cartoon strips, as well as many greeting cards. Jack currently resides in Kansas.